The New TITANIC Returns

The New Titanic Returns
Copyright © 2023 by Burt Jagolinzer

Published in the United States of America
ISBN   Paperback: 978-1-960629-71-5
ISBN   eBook: 978-1-960629-72-2

All rights reserved. No part of this publication may be reproduced, stored in a retrieval system or transmitted in any way by any means, electronic, mechanical, photocopy, recording or otherwise without the prior permission of the author except as provided by USA copyright law.

The opinions expressed by the author are not necessarily those of ReadersMagnet, LLC.

ReadersMagnet, LLC
10620 Treena Street, Suite 230 | San Diego, California, 92131 USA
1.619. 354. 2643 | www.readersmagnet.com

Book design copyright © 2023 by ReadersMagnet, LLC. All rights reserved.

Cover design by Ericka Obando
Interior design by Daniel Lopez

The New TITANIC Returns

BURT JAGOLINZER

ReadersMagnet, LLC

Dedicating this book to my Jo Anne

Pre-Construction:

Great Britain has never forgotten the terrible happenings that took place back in April 1912.
The enormous loss of life, the financial consequences, world-wide embarrassment and the effects on the individuals connected to the disaster still resonates through history.
In his imagination to rebuild the Titanic, this author would have found the special people who would approach this project, with new thinking. confidence to complete the challenge and the financial backing required, in order to make it happen, built with the finest of quality available in today's world.

The New Titanic Returns

A novel by Burt Jagolinzer

The British Broadcasting Corporation (BBC) announced today that The RMS Titanic is to be rebuilt for the White-Star Lines.

Malcolm P. Iceberger, Chairman of the Board of The White Star Line has released the following surprise statement this morning to the BBC News Division, in London:

"It is our privilege to announce to our stock holders, investors, employees, the nation and the world, that the steam-ship ocean liner Titanic will once again take to the seas, as the unfortunate late original vessel had done in its 1912 tragic voyage.

This disaster quickly brought together representatives of the world.

Rules of the oceans were approved since those meetings.

They worked with our people to fine the problems that had caused her demise.

That committee announced to the awaiting world that the problems included the lack of safety equipment, deficiencies in structural and mechanical work, as well as the inadequate training of officers and crew.

The original drafts, drawings and engineering data, together with full details of interior and exterior particulars, are all in our hands.

They will be evaluated and changed to meet the standards of the 21st century today with major changes in structure and safety improvements.

The new ship will actually be longer and slightly wider in size.

The beauty and comfort of the original vessel will be specifically addressed and improved with (once again) the latest of designs and luxury.

As before, this craft will be the largest and greatest afloat, when completed. It will be built by Harland and Wolff, at Belfast Ireland, where the original Titanic had been constructed.

Once again its maiden voyage will begin from Southampton to New York City, as originally planned.

Completion is expected to be in the Spring of 2029, on the anniversary of its original departure, April 15th.

Reservations will become available in London, after January 1st of this next year.

The New Titanic Returns

The cost for the cruise has yet to be determined. Prices will vary, depending on age, personal requirements, position chosen on the ship, one way or round trip and meal selections.

An opening deposit of 500 pounds per person will be required for formal reservations.

Historic History

(The Titanic was an Olympic Class ocean liner, built by Harland & Wolff, in Belfast Ireland to accommodate 2,224 passengers.

Upon completion it was transferred to Southampton, England for the boarding of its maiden run, which was to be Southampton to New York City.

Many of the world's most important individuals were aboard, as were emigrants, hoping to find a new life in "awaiting America".

It had become the largest ship afloat, at that time.

Britain had advertised its coming attraction and people of money and position planned to be there to experience this history-making adventure.

On its second day across the ocean it was advancing south of Newfoundland, when it collided with a large iceberg which ripped a crushing blow to the bottom section of the great ship.

It began to sink.

There were not enough life-boats aboard, only enough for less than one half of the passengers.

Of the 2,224 passengers, only 705 were to survive. They were mostly women and children, who were given priority status when limited boarding.

Some 1,500 and the crew of 90 died in the disaster.

Although the disaster was to be the largest accident in marine history, some good developed from its happening.

The world had not had rules of the oceans. Representatives from around the globe came together to form Safety of Life at Sea (SOLAS) organization which finally created international rules of the oceans.

They focused on safety and better communications for passenger vessels in particular.

It is estimated that millions of lives were to be saved with these new rules, which were immediately put into use throughout the world.)

Final Inspections:

The author's Story

The new Titanic had arrived in port at Southampton.

She had been inspected fourteen times before leaving Belfast, Ireland, where the imposing steamship liner had been totally built.

The material to build her was meticulously improved with the use of new products developed since the disaster.

Safety structures and safety equipment were checked and rechecked to the satisfaction of the inspection committee's important demands.

The new operating crew and their working people were trained and retrained in operational conditions and safety.

The British Government was invited and several members had been assigned to be part of the official delegation aboard the ship.

She now appeared to be ready for boarding.

Preparing for Departure:

Great Britain was proudly selling tickets for their widely advertised event.

Nearly four hundred tickets had been sold in New York City. Their purchasers were mostly people of wealth, who just wanted to be part of this anticipated retrace of world history.

Impressive names like Schleshinger, Forrester, Vanderbuilt, Wang, Bush, Kennedy and Brady were among the American society expected to board the craft.

European dignitaries included the Rothschilds, Onastis, Brookmeyers, Porche, Van Burens, Mellons and Churchills.

The best accommodations were sold out immediately. Only a few second class facilities were still available prior to departure time.

There was a waiting list on all three class tickets when the first whistle was blown.

The New Titanic Returns

The White-Star had now the basic money to secure its financial success.

The price of tickets started at $2,000 US Dollars and ranged to beyond $10,000 US Dollars per person, depending upon requirements requested.

Not all passengers would be returning to Southampton. Many had bargained for just a one-way adventure.

The new ship, having been extended in size, now accommodated 3,010 passengers and a crew of 160.

The London Herald claimed that many of society compared this event more enticing than a trip to the moon.

The Boston Daily Tribute stated that this ship could be considered as a Wonder of the World.

The Bon Voyage

The important nobility in attendance at the Bon Voyage Party included The King of England, dignitaries from Ireland, Scotland, Wales, France, Spain, Germany, The Netherlands, Canada, United States and a long list of representations from other European locations and factions.

There were seven marching bands blasting away and lights flashing in all directions.

Many thousands of on-lookers and vendors covered the entrance to the dockside.

Multi-colored balloons and signs hung from the seven visible decks.

The passengers stood against the heavily supported rails on each level.

The New Titanic Returns

They were waving and shouting as the great liner whistled and shook to the roar of her immense special engines.

Smoke exhibited thick streams of clean omission from the five magnificent stacks placed equally across the gigantic vessel.

The last planks were being taken into the first floor cavity.

Multiple life-boats were seen hanging from each level of the stern.

The viewing stand placed close to the ship was packed with security and attendants.

World history was indeed being made, in front of these dignitaries and on-lookers The great liner's maiden voyage began, as the New Titanic slowly slipped from her port in Southampton, England, ocean bound, heading directly to the United States and the harbor at New York City.

Media and the world had been watching and congratulations were being given to the hundreds of individuals that had been connected to the humungous project, from start to finish.

Getting Ready to Leave

The first bell rang.

It was April 15, 2029 and it was noon.

The New ship was to depart at 5:PM, Southampton time (10:AM in New York City).

It appeared that the New Titanic was ready.

The boarding-planks had continuing activities.

There were vendors pushing assorted boxes, special crates of enclosed food, perishable vegetables and fruits, fresh fish and meat, all moving up the planks.

Just to the right of these items were an unending line of passengers, most with their sundry luggage, all patiently waiting to reach the top and formally -- on to the ship.

The New Titanic Returns

The New Titanic was aglow with the finest of paint, well lit, (even at the noon part of the day).

All of the staff were dressed in colorful British Blue and in enormous numbers that seemed to be everywhere in sight.

They had hired an extra three hundred to perform a variety of added services.

By this time, it appeared that the committee had gone to extremes to make this voyage one, like never before.

The weather was cloudy, about 72-degrees (12-C), with a soft comfortable breeze.

Government official automobiles and police vehicles were spread in all directions. The traffic was routed around the entrance area.

Thousands were walking towards the ship.

The Royal British marching band was stationed at the walking area, playing upbeat military marching music.

Television and media people were kept close to the band location.

Street vendors were prohibited within the entrance complex.

There were six registration booths positioned just prior to the entrance area. The lines were backed up at each booth.

It was a scene of delight for Great Britain and the world.

Burt Jagolinzer

The New Titanic was clearly in the process of preparing for their long planned maiden voyage, that many thought could never be accomplished again.

The Beginning Part-2

Manny Fairfield, age 53, grew up in Portsmouth, England.

He attended Clarke-Regent School of Economics, graduating number three in his class.

After serving four years in the British Air Force, he began work at The Rolls Royce Company in their engine department.

There he met his wife-to be, Caroline, who was a secretary in one of their main offices. They married the following year.

Seven months into the marriage Caroline ran away to Switzerland with her Roman Catholic Priest.

Manny suffered the loss of Caroline and he became fearful of women.

His marriage ruined, he departed Rolls-Royce and wondered around London.

Manny's medical doctor recommended that he consider taking a trip somewhere.

He discovered The New Titanic adventure and thought it might be good for his problem.

When the day came to board, Manny arrived an hour late and nearly missed the ship's departure.

Claude Williamson and his wife Sarah came from Newfoundland, Canada.

They had won the lottery, collecting some two million dollars.

While touring Europe they had heard about The Titanic adventure and decided to immediately purchase tickets in first class.

They had just left Italy and had flown to Heathrow Airport when a bomb scare took place at the airport.

Everything was stopped and they were delayed for almost eight hours.

Wisely, Claude telephoned the ship, expecting to possibly arriving late for departure.

They had told them that the original departure time had now been changed, adding five more hours to accommodate late arriving vendors and some individuals.

The New Titanic Returns

Claude and Sarah finally reached the departure area and stopped for a cup of coffee.

It was Kenny's Pub, located about two blocks from the New Titanic birth.

The coffee was not that great, but the homemade English muffins were delightful.

The Beginning Part 3

Nancy Burgess and her half-sister Norma Burgess had been working for Lloyds of London in their research division. They were both twenty-six years of age.

They had each come from their father's different sexual affairs, with birthdays only four days apart.

When their father finally married one of them, he was able to bring the girls together a short time later.

The two half-sisters became very close.

The New Titanic advertisement caught their attention and it prompted them to take a two-week vacation, including the voyage aboard this New Titanic.

Their trip would include some shopping and touring of New York City and then fly back to London at the end.

They registered "Advanced Second Class", which gave them access to the social life of the first-class, without the fancy suites that came with the first-class accommodations.

Russell Steinhoff was born in Colon, West Germany, in 1959, making him sixty-two years old at this time.

After attending Kraus Marine Technical School in Bremen, Germany he accepted a five-year stint, as an officer aboard the ocean liner Berliner, which sailed the high seas of the Mediterranean.

Upon becoming a registered Captain, he applied for a job with the Seaman Oil Company. He was to stay with them, leading ships throughout the world for many years.

When the New Titanic opened their search for veteran Captains, Russell was among the first to respond, seeking a position.

The New Titanic commission immediately hired Captain Steinhoff as part of their control-team.

Russell had never married and had only two affairs of any significance.

His pay for this adventure, back and forth aboard the New Titanic was beyond any other compensation he had ever received.

Russell was thrilled about the challenge and the spectacular pay.

Burt Jagolinzer

He arrived at the dockside early in the morning.

When boarded, he was assigned a very fancy suite on the upper deck, not far from the control room of the ship.

The Beginning Part 5

Russian SVR representative Liani Zeel was registered for the trip months ago.

(In 1991 the Russian KGB was broken into two parts, the SVR, or the foreign intelligence service, and the FSB branch)

He was trained for many years by his government, having served in several special encounters with foreign agents, spies and criminals.

Liani was a veteran soldier and military leader who had paid his dues many years earlier.

He was fifty-six years old, twice married, now single, without children.

Among his roles on the voyage were to take pictures and to examine the controlling brains of the ship.

He was to return to Moscow as soon as possible after completing the roundtrip back to Southampton.

His Superiors, back in Russia, were to be waiting for his personal report.

The Beginning: Part-1

The villages around Southampton were packed with individuals who had come to the area, some for just a look at the liner or to observe the attention that had assembled for the great advertised event.

Rosaline Bosh, or Roz as many would call her, was the daughter of Pierre and Darlene Bosh of Alcura, Mexico. Pierre had amassed a fortune in the manufacture of women's accessories that were sold around the world.

Her family was believed to be worth many billions in today's economy.

When she married Terrance (or Terry) Gates, she was a millionaire-ist.

Terrance had come from San Francisco, California, where his mother, who had inherited millions from the Hearst estate, due to her faithful years serving the Hearst family, had set up a living trust for her only child, Terrance.

Roz and Terry had met during their junior year at University of Southern California (USC).

The good-looking couple was quickly put together.

When they graduated from USC, two years later, they decided to get married the following April 11th.

Daddy Bosh wanted the wedding to be in Mexico, but Roz objected.

She chose Las Vegas, as a compromise, which was one of Daddy's favorite play cities.

While Roz and her mother Darlene were planning the wedding, Terry was considering their honeymoon trip.

Terry had read about the new Titanic and quickly booked tickets, from New York and a flight to England, the day before.

When Daddy Bosh heard about Terry's plans, he immediately told everyone that Mommy and Daddy would go on that adventure, as well.

Terry was not so pleased to hear the announcement, but, Roz thought it would be OK. She told Terry to go along with their plans.

And so, the wedding took place at The Royal-Turner Hotel, one of the newest hotels on the strip in Las Vegas.

Three hundred and nine people witnessed the joyous wedding, which included a special private show, featuring Albert and Cecile Dupont, the latest singing sensations, just off Broadway.

The New Titanic Returns

The wedding party took up the entire top floor of the hotel.

Dick Lupino's fourteen-piece orchestra played until 2:00AM. It became Society's featured April event.

The newly Weds and her parents flew to New York City for the first leg of their trip to Southampton.

Their flight out of Kennedy International Airport was delayed almost five hours.

Fortunately, they found a fancy restaurant at the airport to have dinner and to waste some four of the five hours.

The newly-weds flew economy coach, while her parents went first class.

When they arrived at Heathrow Airport in London a hired vehicle was waiting to take them across Britain to the outskirts of Southampton.

They were to spend the night at The Sovereign-Southampton Resort.

Like everything in the area it had been sold-out well in advance.

There, in the hotel they were to meet, by accident, Jules Madison, the coal-mine magnate from Dublin, Ireland.

Jules just happen to have made reservations for The Titanic several months ago and was traveling first-class on the ship.

Jules and Roz's father, Pierre Bush, hit it off quickly and was to spend several hours in the lounge of the hotel talking business and politics.

Roz's mother, Darlene, was not very happy about her husband spending the time with this unknown gentleman.

Jules Madison had been born into a coal-connected family. His father had worked many years employed by The House of Common Coal Company, which owned over thirty mines throughout Ireland.

Business was so good that the company couldn't keep important records and happenings at many of the mines, particularly those in the southern part of Ireland, which amounted to twelve mines.

Ownership regarded Jules's father, Peter Madison, as a valued and honest administrator.

They approached him and offered him a deal, to manage their southern mines for ten years, and you'll be awarded 50% percent ownership, at that time.

Peter Madison not only moved his family to Dublin and took the job, but was to remain there for some thirty-five years.

After the first ten years he gained 50% percent ownership, as they promised. On his 12th year he was to buy out the other 50% per cent, to gain complete ownership.

During year 15 he purchased 1/3rd ownership in two other of their northern mines.

By the 18th year he had amassed the entire ownership of The House of Common Company, and was worth millions.

Young Jules was brought up at attending private prep schools and entered Oxford.

He was a cricket champion and received many awards before graduation.

Jules began taking over his father's businesses.

Three years later he married Juliette O'Landy from Leeds. Their daughter, Tigress was born the following year.

Unfortunately, his wife was severely hit by a wild horse and became paralyzed in most of her body. She was moved to a helpful home where she could be taken care of by trained-devoted people.

Juliette wanted Jules to find another woman who might be able to take her place in his life. Jules refused, saying "You and you alone will always be my woman".

Finally, their daughter Tigress insisted that he take The Titanic trip to get away from his problems.

He finished telling Pierre his story, excused himself and went to bed in his plush hotel room.

Father Paul O'Grammit had been born in Rosemont, Scotland in 1938. He was now 84 years old, and in pretty good health.

When he was eighteen he entered the seminary to become a Priest.

He was to serve his religion faithfully for nearly sixty-six years,

His nieces and nephews bought him a ticket on The New Titanic.

He was very excited about the trip, and to finally visit the United States of America.

A black sedan had driven him to dockside this very morning. The driver was apparently a member of his Order, which had approved of his trip.

Dressed in appropriate black suit and white collar, and holding the handle of his black suitcase he began boarding the first deck of The New Titanic

The Beginning Part: 4

Peter Cummings had obtained the last ticket on the ship.

Because he was by-himself the final "odd" ticket had been available since yesterday. Needless to say, he was indeed lucky.

Cummings was from San Diego, California, 48 years old and a divorcee of four marriages.

Peter was an electrician by trade, but never holding on to jobs throughout his twenty-five years at the trade.

He had been visiting his aging grandmother in Belfast, Ireland when he had seen advertisement for The New Titanic.

Peter told his grandmother he would get on board. She didn't believe him and laughed when he left her the day before he had arrived in Southampton.

Smartly, Peter telephoned his grandmother to tell her of his success and that he was now aboard the ship. His grandmother couldn't believe it.

Wendi Cegall was America's Ambassador to Eastern Lithuania.

She had graduated from Arizona State University with a Degree in Political Science.

After accepting a job working for the American-Embassy in Paris, she was appointed Ambassador by then President Barron Trump

She was on vacation and decided to go back to America on Britain's latest luxury liner today.

Wendi was twenty-nine years old and single.

Her mother would be waiting in New York City to return her to their family home in Framingham, Massachusetts.

Wendi's best friend, Ruthi Sugarberger, was accompanying her mother at the New York dockside. They had not seen Wendi for nearly two years.

Titanic Cruising Day-1

Each room in first class had flowers, chocolates and a bottle of French Wine waiting for them.

The rooms were prepared carefully with eloquent colors throughout. There were towels everywhere and plenty of them. The lights were bright with the latest configurations about them.

The air-conditioning was perfectly set and noiseless. Maid service would be offered to the occupants twice per day. A button, next to the bathroom was to be used to call for maid service. Portions of the maid service would be completed by an accompanying robot, programmed to quickly handle an array of individual services.

One's registration-card closes and unlocks the doors.

Second class and advanced-second class enjoy several of the services of first class, but within smaller rooms and with limited luxury.

Third class is rather basic but without the special services offered in the other classes. Their rooms are quite small, but adequate for the voyage.

On each floor there is living-room like facilities that are set to accommodate each passenger. Computers, game rooms, cafes, dining rooms and an entertainment event hall, compliments their sleeping locations.

Each floor also has a casino with the latest of gambling available.

The Titanic has two swimming pools, both on the top deck. One is quite large and the other smaller one to accommodate children and the handicapped. A gym and workout facility is smartly located next to the larger pool.

The top deck also has seven stores for shopping, including an expanded book store, technical parts and repair shop, beauty salons, hair dressers and a clothing-bizarre with the latest of fashions.

Each of the three main floors schedule meal time callings by numbers, one, two or three.

The top deck has a special entrance to the Operation Control Complex, to be referred to as OCC, with built-in top security.

At the stern of the ship perched high into a rafter is a helicopter, to be used only on emergency.

The Captain, other ranking officers and several special assistants are instructed to be regularly walking about the ship, reassuring the security, normal operations and to answer questions that may be of importance to their passengers. This is a 24-hour vigil that brings the leadership closer to the average passenger and adds to the uniqueness of the trip.

Captain Russell Steinhoff is first to leave the OCC and visit the upper deck.

Among his first meeting was a group, which included Father Paul O'Grammit.

The Captain began, "Good afternoon Father, I'm Captain Russ and who might you be, my good Father?"

"I'm Father Paul...and very excited about being here for this journey", he responded.

Other members of the group together shouted, "Glad to have you.

Good luck for a safe and wonderful cruise"

The Captain moved on across the deck.

There at the deep end of the large swimming pool stood young Wendi Ceagall. She smiled and waved to the moving Captain, as he strode by her.

The New Titanic had left Southampton and was well into the sea before the Captain had announced to his staff that he was about to take the first walk and meet some of the passengers.

"I'll be back in about fifteen minutes", he stated.

And he began his first walk (or watch) upon the ship.

Tita Cruising Day-1, Part B

Pierre and Darlene Bosh had just arrived into their first class states room when his personal cell phone rang and rang.

He put down his hand held computer on the table adjacent to the entrance way. "It's probably my mother", he shouted.

No, it was his sister Grace, to tell them that their mother of ninety-two had taken a stroke. "She'll recover, the old bitch", complained Grace.

Grace and their mother had been apart for the last twenty years, not even talking to each other.

Sister Grace was very close to her brother Pierre and Darlene and she knew that Pierre had to be informed about his mother, even on their special holiday cruise.

"Thank you for ruining my vacation", he responded. After being updated on his mother's current situation, he ended the conversation.

The New Titanic Returns

Darlene immediately criticized Pierre for his response to his sister.

"OK, I'm sorry but… she's still my mother and the news affected my response. I'll apologize to Grace later", he returned.

"Listen Pierre, this place is beautiful. I'm glad we're here, aren't you?", Darlene began.

The newly wedded couple had chosen the advanced-second class accommodations, on the level below her parents.

Their registration card would not open their room door. "Would you believe this?" Terry cursed.

"I'll have to go to the office to get a new card…or something", he continued.

Roz responded, "I'll stay on this outside chair until your return".

Her new husband, Terry Gates, walked briskly down the hallway toward the ship's second floor office.

Peter Cummings had already unpacked in his advanced-second class room and had decided to stroll the ship to see what and who might interest him.

Two doors down towards the bow was a very pretty young gal sitting, by herself, on a chair.

He introduced himself quickly and presented his name to her. "And who might you be?" he requested.

"I am Roz Gates, and I am waiting for my new husband Terry, who has gone to fetch a decent registration card, so we can enter our room." she responded.

"If I can be of service to you, am but two doors down this way. It's been a pleasure to have met you this day", he returned.

Peter immediately walked away.

He began talking to himself that this lady was quite beautiful, young and happy. This is the kind of a woman I need in my life.

Maybe I might find one aboard this liner?

Titanic Cruising Day-1, Part D

Claude and Sarah Williamson, from Newfoundland, Canada, who had won the 2 million-dollar lottery, were among the first to come aboard.

They had first-class accommodations reserved and were welcomed like the others.

The registration card opened their door as promised and they too were delighted with the room and amenities that came with it.

Claude slipped in the bathroom and bruised his right elbow. He cursed his new shoes for the slippery introduction to the bathroom.

Sarah saw this slip as an indication to what may follow for them.

Claude didn't like her verbal outcry. "Be positive and don't let this little incident spoil our great vacation", he responded.

"Let's unpack and change our clothes for the evening meal. We have the third dining call." Sarah returned.

They began unpacking their individual travel bags.

When Claude finished empting his personal clothing, he sat down on a brand-new expensive-looking leather chair and quickly placed his feet upon the matching leather foot-stool.

Within minutes he was fast asleep. Sarah continued with her dressing.

Titanic Cruising Day-1 - "Evening"

The Captain planned the first evening entertainment on all three passenger levels.

On the first upper level, which includes all first-class passengers was entertained by a French Comedian and the new Neal Hefti Orchestra, with dancing.

The second floor entertainment included a London magician and the Jimmy Parcella Society Orchestra, with Clara Pinkerton, as featured vocalist. Dancing was also encouraged.

Entertainment on the third floor included the romantic songs by the great tenor soloist, Carmen Shwartzberger, from East Berlin, with the Lois-Von German Orchestra.

All dinner seating individuals began introducing each other around their various tables.

Single people were seated in an area, with ten per table, and were placed randomly.

Jules Madison sat between Norma and Nancy Burgess.

Peter Cummings was placed next to Liani Zeel on one side and Wendi Cegall on the other side.

They all began talking to one another, while the music played in the background.

Cummings talked his way into a dance with Wendi Cegall and they continued dancing for three straight numbers.

When they sat down Wendi asked Peter Cummings if he had a woman in his life. Peter responded, "No, but you could be possibly a new one".

"Don't give me that bit. I've heard a lot of comebacks at that inquiry. But remember, we hardly know each other. I'm game, to go a little further." Wendy returned.

"Then, after desert, how about another dance?", he rebounded.

"Yes, that would be alright. Let's eat cake and ice cream first", Wendi finalized.

Liani Zeel, overhearing the two dancers' remarks stated, "Back in Russia there would be no conversation like that."

Peter Cummings returned, "That's why we are glad not to be in Russia". He finished his remarks with a smile.

The New Titanic Returns

The two dancers spent the remaining hours dancing, imbibing and exchanging background information to each other.

When the evening was over Peter walked Wendi to her door and reached across for a kiss. Wendi received the kiss quite by surprise, but openly indicated that she fully enjoyed the gesture.

Liani Zeel had gone to bed several hours prior.

Titanic Cruising Day - 1 - "Evening" - A

Captain Russell had dismissed his upper staff, allowing them to get some sleep until the morning change of leadership at the helm of the giant ship.

He knew that he would not be able to sleep during the first night of the journey and decided to stay in the OCC.

The ship continued to perform well, as it did during trials (and its trip from Ireland to Southampton). Thank God, as the world would be watching and waiting for nothing less than good news from this venture throughout.

A waiter brought the Captain two cups of strong coffee, without additions. He drank a lot of coffee and just loved its taste and aroma. It would also keep him widely awake during the long early morning hours at the helm.

The New Titanic Returns

There were two subordinates in the OCC with him, at all times. Both were drinking tea, like the good Englishmen that they were. The waiter had brought them their drinks earlier.

One of the subordinates was a former British Lancer in Great Britain's special division of their Army, who had retired and was hired immediately upon his application.

Martin Glory was his name and he was thirty-seven years old, and single.

The other subordinate was Tom Tarnish, an English soccer star, who had broken his leg during the finals of the World Cup. Tom was certainly a Star among athletes and their followers. He was quite handsome, at twenty-six and divorced.

He too was hired upon application, due to his clean background.

The evening and early morning shift in the OCC appeared to have gone by quite quickly. The sun began rising in the east.

Titanic Cruising Day - 2

Norma and Nancy Burgess arose at 6:00AM. They quickly washed and dressed and were ready to investigate and enjoy what they could find aboard the vessel.

The early sun was beating down on the top floor of the moving ship.

Several tourists were already into their bathing suits and beginning to soak up the warm and comfortable rays. They were decked out in modern lounge chairs facing the eastern early morning sunrise.

Nancy wanted to go back to their room and change into bathing ware but Norma convinced her to wait until after breakfast.

Instead they continued walking the upper deck beyond the two swimming pools and to inspect the windows of the closed stores that lined the rear portion of the deck. The signs in the stores indicated their openings were to take place at 9:00AM.

The New Titanic Returns

Nancy discovered Theresa's Pot Luck, an up-scale fashion outlet, displaying colorful, eloquent and high quality brands of women's youthful selections.

She screamed at Norma, telling her that this store would be a must, when it opened today. Norma nodded her head and verbally agreed.

They finished their inspection of the area, returned to their room and made their final adjustments for the up and coming breakfast.

A waitress, carrying breakfast to a honeymooning couple on the second deck had fallen at the base of the far stairwell.

Coffee, juice, toast and eggs were scattered all around the bottom area.

She had hot coffee and pieces of toast, down the front of her work uniform. She was crying and was a mess.

Pierre Bosh had just left his room to hopefully find an early morning Newspaper, when he came upon the waitress and the obvious accident.

"Don't cry", he blurted, "I'll call the desk for help and they will surely get you back in shape quite quickly".

"I'll wait with you until help arrives. My name is Pierre, what is your name?", he continued.

"I'm Georgina, but everyone calls me George". she returned, wiping her eyes. "Thank you for your help. I will need to change clothes and get a new platter of breakfast for the awaiting couple."

Meanwhile, the two individuals exchanged information and an immediate friendship began to form. Amazingly the chemistry between them brought out laughter to supplement the entertainment that arose.

When the ship officials arrived to clean up the mess Pierre offered to escort Georgina to her room towards the back of the OCC complex, where much of the staff was being housed.

"I hope we will meet again…and for you to meet my wife and family. I'm sure that they would love to meet you. And by-the-way, be careful walking around this ship in the future." Pierre finished.

Titanic Evening, Day-2

Guido Bassorelli had been placed aboard, long before most of the passengers had climbed aboard the vessel.

Two men, driving a new sleek Italian Maserati had released Guido into the front of this special ship.

He was told to "act your usual way, and don't let anyone stop you. Big Georgio, and the boys, will be there to meet you in New York. Everything on board has been paid-for by a credit card, from a client. Just sign your name. Have a good ride".

They had driven from Heathrow in London since early in the morning. He was exhausted.

Guido was a professional pick-pocket expert. He came from Geneva, but had set the record in Venice, with thirty-one picks during last year's New Year's Eve. It was a good way to start the New Year.

He had been averaging twelve picks per day, and considered to be among the top ten pickers in Italy alone.

New York was awaiting him.

Big Georgio, during his last visit to Palermo, had heard about Guido, and had asked to borrow him for six months.

The local boys decided to give him the six months with Big Georgio, for 10% of the total collection.

It was supposed to be "A deal, made in Heaven".

Only time would tell.

His room was on the third floor, facing the steps, connecting the rest of the floors and access to the deck.

After unpacking his muscle and assorted hardware, he decided to catch up on his sleep. He went right to bed and slept through the rest of the first day.

When he awoke on the second afternoon, he immediately washed and dressed.

He was now ready to explore the ship, starting with the upper deck area.

On his way up the stairs toward the deck, he passed a well-dressed waiter, who was carrying two bottles of wine and some cheese.

Guido moved slightly to his left and lifted his wallet quite easily.

The New Titanic Returns

He had made his first pick, on the way to the top of the ship.

Nearly two hundred dollars were inside, plus his credit card.

Guido didn't do credit cards, nor did he keep wallets.

So, at the top of deck he spotted a wide table, situated out into the walking area, and he quickly deposited it, facing easy exposure.

Guido slowly walked away.

Even though it was already the second evening, it appeared to be a successful beginning for Guido, aboard the new Titanic.

Titanic Evening Day - 2 (continued)

Georgina, the waitress, was walking around the deck, later in the evening, when she bumped into Pierre Bosh once again.

She offered him a free drink. He quickly responded, "My card includes free drinks anyway. But I'll take a whiskey-sour, if you please".

About ten minutes later she appeared, carrying his chosen drink, "I've added some cheese and crackers for you", she communicated.

"Please come and meet me, when your shift is over", Pierre responded.

"Thank you, but I don't know whether it is permissible to socialize with passengers, or not", she returned. "But, I'll do it anyway... about nine o'clock, right here. I'll see you soon", she finished.

Off she went, headed towards the stairs.

Pierre was joined by his wife Darlene Bosh, and the newly wedded, daughter Roz and Son-In-Law, Terry Gates.

They too ordered drinks, and their chatter included assessments of the magnificent new ship.

Their experiences and opinions were quite favorable, indicating their happiness for the sail, so far.

When they opted to break up their gathering at 8:30 PM, Pierre announced that he would stay here for a short time to further unwind.

And, of course 9:PM approached, and Georgina arrived.

She was out of her waitress uniform, and into a beautiful sundress, of bright yellow, with a scooped neck. A gold necklace, with the hanging letter G sparkling on its chain complimented the dress

Her hair had been rearranged, and gold earrings were dangling from her ears.

She had matching handbag and shoes of off-yellow, to match her other clothes.

Her confidence and smile added to her looks.

She was a different woman than the waitress Pierre had helped a few hours earlier.

He was wonderfully surprised, and appeared amazed.

"Your beauty and youth are extraordinary, to say the least. I am taken by your change. You must have many men attracted to you." he asked.

"No, men usually want me for my looks. I want a man, who would want me for my brains, values and personal uniqueness. I have yet to find, such a man.

But, your politeness and help, has drawn me to you, even though you are supposedly married."

"Wow" he returned, "Yes, I am married, but not happily so.

We had been apart for several years, and have kept together for our daughter, and her just completed marriage.

For quite some time it had not been working.

She rekindled an old high school romance, at a reunion about ten years ago. And they have been meeting quite often since then.

I told my friends that I would wait until after the wedding to do anything.

But, I am now ready to leave the marriage.

She should be happy, and go live with her old flame.

My life would immediately be opened to new adventure and possibilities." he completed.

"Let's get to know each other, and see where it leads us. You seem like an interesting man.

I'll start, for a bit, and then you can begin, as well. Is this OK?" she returned. "Yes, I would enjoy that. Please begin." Pierre answered.

Titanic Morning - Day - 3

Members of the Russian SVR don't usually like being pickpocketed by strangers, let alone while on a holiday ocean liner.

Guido Bassorelli appeared to have been working quite hard. He had had four picks since day two.

His coffers had been filled to the tune of one thousand U.S. Dollars and a bit more.

Russian agent, Liani Zeel, with the insignia Z on his cap, began searching for the thief.

Zeel was considered an expert in location and pursuit.

His keen eyes and quick reflexes aided him in location. He was determined to catch the culprit.

Zeel had reported his loss to the ship Captain, who had already received news of the other three's similar happenings.

The Captain's security people had been told of the situation, and were keeping their eyes alerted.

Zeel promised the Captain that he would be searching as well.

Smartly, Guido was to stay low until the next day, to keep away from the searchers, who would have begun their ship-wide coverage, looking for him (or them).

Let us remember, Guido was supposed to be a veteran picker, with much European experience.

The thousand-dollar hoist was far from his daily objectives. This man was a seasoned professional.

Titanic Evening - Day - 3

Alexander Reed, from Belfast Ireland, had stolen soap, shampoo, conditioner and towels from three rooms that were being set up for arriving guests on the second floor. (The name "Titanic" had been well printed on each item).

Reed had hoped to sell the items after completing the trip. He had also thought that his collection could be enlarged before leaving the ship.

Coincidental to the timing of Guido's three pocket pixs, Reed kept looking back, after stealing his initial collection.

When the security forces and the Russian, Liani Zeel spotted Reed walking quite gingerly along the second floor corridor, they collectively shouted for him to stop.

Reed immediately thought they had discovered his stealing and began to run towards the end of the corridor.

Liani Zeel opened fire and Reed was taken down.

When they approached the falling body, they discovered that Reed had been killed. He laid there in a pile of his own blood.

Security people weren't sure what to do. They decided to take Liani Zeel to Security Headquarters. Zeel cooperated with the request.

Liani Zeel had shot and killed Reed, after fair warning. What should enforcement do to him, at this time? And, how will this be handled?

Word of the murder traveled around the ship.

The Officials were about to report to ship passengers via the speaker system from the control room.

Needless to say, people were stunned to have had a murder aboard this special maiden-voyage.

A representative from the British Government, Sgt. Manuel Transmission was stationed on this ship for just a situation.

He was to make decisions like this. But if he wasn't sure of a particular action, he was trained to communicate with his office, back in London, for their view, before actually committing to a final decision on the issue.

And so, Sgt. Manual phoned his office for their advice, "Take away all his weapons and hold him at bay", he responded.

"Don't let him go freely for the rest of the trip. We will be waiting for him in New York, when you arrive", he continued

The ship officials calmed down.

Things began to return to normal.

Titanic Cruising Day - 1, Part C

The two half-sisters, Nancy and Norma Burgess had stopped for a drink upon entering the ship. They chose the café on the second level.

They began sipping glasses of Rose' wine, that came with small cookies. The cookies fascinated them.

"The wine is quite good and the cookies are delicious. What a great start to our vacation." remarked Norma.

"Let's toast to a safe and fun time aboard the New Titanic", answered Nancy. They put their glasses high and the toast was properly made.

When they finished their drinks and signed for the purchases, with their room number, they began walking down towards the stern, looking for their room number.

The New Titanic Returns

The Russian SVR agent, Liani Zeel was coming from the opposite direction. He was wearing a cap with the insignia Z, boldly on the face of the cap.

Norma spotted the cap and yelled to him, "What is the Z for?"

In his broken English he responded, "My name is Zeel", and continued passing by the two young women.

Zeel had just completed his first walk around the ship, taking in many of the important locations on each level. This information could have affect for decisions made later in the cruise

Nancy and Norma found their room and entered without problem.

They quickly decided that the room and the amenities were more than adequate, and that their decision to take this level was a smart economic move.

On their desk was a large card indicating that they would be seated for meals during the first servings, meaning 11:30 AM, and 5:30 PM, considered to be the early dining.

They could now plan their time and dress for each day.

Jules Madison sat on the couch in his first class room, with a cup of decafe' in his hand. He was reading his assignment for dining, which gave him the last seating, 1:30 PM and 8:30PM.

"I only hope that they don't run out of food when get there", he said to himself, with a smile.

His daughter Tigress had sent him a message, wishing him a great time and hoping that he meets some nice people to help him with his ongoing problem.

Jules began dressing for dinner which was still several hours away.

He wanted to feel dressed properly and to slowly work his way towards the dining area.

"Maybe I'll buy myself a local newspaper to read during my wait", he said to himself.

Waiting next to the dining area on the second level was Manny Fairfield.

He had been assigned to the late serving time as well. Manny sat on a colorful lounge chair near the door entrance, with a book in his hand.

While reading, he looked up from the book and spotted Jules Madison just about to sit down next to him, on a cushioned rocking chair.

"Don't let me bother you from reading, I'm Jules Madison, from down the hall", he submitted.

"Oh, I'd rather talk to someone than read anyway", he responded.

"My name is Manny Fairfield, from Portsmouth, England"., he countered.

They began a conversation that lasted nearly two hours and became trip buddies.

A server approached them and they ordered drinks, Jules a martini and Manny a beer.

Soon the doors to the dining hall opened and the previous diners began leaving the hall.

When the last one departed Jules and Manny decided to go in.

They carried with them their unfinished drinks and were seated by the waiters.'

Jules and Manny were at the same table but at opposite ends. But they were to meet the same people and consume the same food.

Fresh North-Sea flounder or native goose was at the top of the menu, with assorted vegetables and ending with homemade apple pie.

Around their table were Doctor and Mrs. Henry Berlin, II, from

Auckland, New Zealand, and Vivian Buckley, their daughter in-law, Conrad Booper, a noted radio guru and Donald J. Peanutbutler, a London hairdresser.

They all seemed happy and glad to be aboard. They were probably hungry, as well.

Titanic Cruising Day - 2, Part 1

It was the second day that Jules Madison and Manny Fairfield had met.

They continued to discuss business, the stock market and a number of world transactions that were happening on a daily basis.

Manny mentioned that he had a citrus farm to sell in Mesa, Arizona.

"I've owned it for nearly seven years. It nets me $14,000 each year, during each of the last four years.

I'd sell it for twenty-eight thousand to an enterprising investor. It runs by itself.

Just one man manages, and he hires four or five local people to help pick, twice a year.

The distributors buy up the harvest at a good price each year.

Would you be interested?", Manny declared.

"I'd give you twenty-five thousand for it RIGHT NOW!", Jules responded.

"You got yourself a deal. Let's shake", answered Manny.

They reached across the table and shook hands to seal the deal.

"I'll have my lawyer draw up the transaction. It could be ready next week.

He'll mail it out to you immediately.", Manny continued,

Brett Williams had made a small fortune washing windows in Philadelphia, Pittsburgh and Baltimore.

He had sold his growing business for twelve million dollars, at the age of twenty-seven.

At age twenty he married his young girlfriend Mildred and they had added two young children, now ages six and four. They had been traveling Europe when Mildred spotted the ad in the London newspaper.

They quickly made reservations on this new Titanic.

The Williams' were settled in first-class accommodations.

New Titanic Cruising Day - 2, Part 1

Rough seas began pounding the ship.

The designers had increased her weight and other configurations to help offset the expected pounding.

The Titanic continued safely on her scheduled movement across the vast pond before her.

No complaints from passengers had reached the controlling team.

But ice burgs had not yet been sighted.

The temperature on the top deck lowered, approaching the freezing point. No one was swimming in the pools.

Three floors of casino participants produced much revenue for the ship's investors. There were very few winners among them.

The big event for the day was the anticipation of the Captain's special dinner, to be hosted by the Captain and his staff.

Live music, Champagne and selected beef was to top the evening. (Passengers were asked to dress appropriately for the event)

Dance instructors were assigned to each floor, offering a lesson or two to those who might enjoy the opportunity.

It was to be a very special evening, possibly the highlight of the voyage.

New Titanic, Part

Amanda Stone and Billy-Bob Hudson became an item.

She had grown up in Serina, Indiana, where her father, Alexander Stone had controlled an automobile repair shop, continuing spinning-back speedometers on used cars.

The Feds caught up with him and sent him to jail for ten years.

His family suffered socially and Amanda and her family were forced to leave the community.

Amanda flew to London, England and set-up residency when British authorities approached her to either give up her United States citizenship and become a Brit, or leave the country.

She found a chance to join the new Titanic, employed as the manager of the women's only boutique aboard the ship.

The pay was good and she was given two other women to help run the business with her.

Billy-Bob came from Hudson, New Hampshire, where his family roots go back to the Mayflower. (His great great-grandfather had helped build the Mayflower, back in England).

His Uncle Tom became New Hampshire's first Governor-elected (where all previous Governors had all been appointed).

The automobile, The Hudson, was named after his Grandfather.

(Many people think he might have been connected to the famous explorer, Henry Hudson).

Billy-Bob was employed on the ship, as the maintenance chief.

They were to meet, when Billy-Bob visited the boutique to check on potential maintenance considerations.

When they met… it became love, at first sight.

Other members of the ship crew had all noted their on-going affair.

The Captain asked the crew to leave them alone.

ADD TO: New Titanic

Train magnate Alexander Bosko, majority stockholder of the New York Central Line, was working a deal with Cocco Lee, Chairman of the Board, of JAPSOL, a Japanese manufacturer of precision fast-trains, for thirty sleek platinum, state-of-the-arts, passenger trains, to be delivered in the year 2030. The cost of the acquisition was to be in the trillion-billions of US currency.

The New Titanic Returns

On board was thirteen members of the Cleveland Jr. Community College, which had won their fourth year in a row the Division-I Men's Basketball Championship.

International Chess Champion, Boris Jagolinski, was doing his best in the first level living area. Challengers were arriving from all over the ship. His wife Sally was bored and very upset with him. It was supposed to have been a vacation for them.

Movie mongrel, Sidney Vonderburg, was giving out discount movie coupons to those he would meet along his daily walks.

New Titanic Page

It was early on the third morning when the Captain was apprised that icebergs had been sighted on the right side of the ship.

He immediately communicated with everyone, recommending that they view the sightings.

They were assured that this ship could breakthrough any iceberg safely, not like the original ship experienced.

New Titanic, Part

Jeanie Cole was 5'7: inches tall, dirty-blond hair and gorgeous

She had been appointed assistant manager at the ship's women boutique, on the upper deck.

Jeanie was about to be handcuffed.

She was being arrested by ship's security people.

Fifteen minutes ago witnesses had seen her fighting with a British sailor.

They had watched her shake off his advancement, dislodge his hands, that had been around her, and tossed him on to the railing perch that was nearby.

The sailor lost his balance and plunged over the close railing into the ocean below him.

Movement of the New Titanic made saving him impossible. He was quickly "lost at sea".

Everyone in the area screamed.

Jeanie couldn't wait to discuss the incident. She was expected at the boutique, to relive her boss, the manager.

It had taken place on the forward top deck across from the side entrance to the control facilities.

Jeanie immediately left the scene and reported to the boutique, where her manager was awaiting her scheduled arrival.

After entering the store, right behind her were security authorities.

(Jeannie had been a trained graduate black-belt and certainly wouldn't have allowed a British sailor man-handle her. Would it be considered "self-defense"?)

The investigation was sure to follow.

New Titanic Page

Rough seas began pounding the ship. Mist and wind disturbed the top deck.

The designers had increased her weight and configurations to help offset the expected pounding.

The New Titanic safely continued her scheduled movement across the vast pond.

To date, there hadn't been any passenger complaints. And, there had not been sightings of icebergs, so far.

The temperature on the top deck lowered and it approached freezing. There weren't swimmers in the pools.

Thee level of casino participants produced much income for the ship's investors. As expected, there were few winners.

The Captain and his staff had been walking throughout the ship meeting many of the passengers on all the levels.

The second day had come to a close and there were no new signs of the pickpocketer. Security people were still watching closely for movements in all directions.

New Titanic Page

Would you believe that a guy was going door-to-door selling Fulla-Brush? (If he worked hard he could probably exceed his monthly sales quota on board this ship) Norman Churchill, one of the young members of the Churchill Family aboard claims he spotted a UFO (Unidentified Flying Object) during the second night.

He said the object tailed-off to the west and disappeared.

The pickpocketer had actually picked some nine pockets in the first three days but only four had reported their losses.

He was amazed and with $1,700 US dollars in his jacket pocket liner. That being the case, he thought he could easily double his numbers before reaching New York. Only time would tell.

Security had devised a trap to catch the thief.

Teresa Bishop (veteran security worker) would display an easy pick from her shoulder handbag. Chief Carman Smith would follow behind her to catch the pick. It was to start immediately.

Sure enough, our thief spotted her set-up and approached her from behind. He took the bait and went for the pick.

(However, he was one of the finest in Italy for a reason.)

He smartly tapped her on the shoulder and presented her with the pick, and stated, "Be careful, as there have been several people who have lost items."

Chief Smith watched and listened closely but couldn't make an arrest.

He had outfoxed them.

But Chief Smith still thought this guy……as suspicious.

"We'll follow him, just to be sure", he contributed.

Yes, they finally caught him.

He was about to pick the pocket of Reginald Pearce, Assistant Manager of the White Star Line, who was just about to climb the stairs to the upper deck.

Chief Carman Smith from security had been following him and quickly made the arrest.

The culprit escaped when Smith fumbled with the handcuffs.

Smith didn't even get the chance to obtain his name. Wow. But he at least now knows his appearance.

Chief Smith had to relate the incident to all the other security people.

While being embarrassed he was able to state, "At least, we know what he looks like. We'll pass his features to everyone aboard. And, by the way, he didn't possess any weapons, and appeared very easy going. We should be able to catch him, now that we have this information".

Lost and Found: Found Reported: a women's diamond bracelet, a man's upscale Rolex wrist watch and a full box of condoms, found at various locations on the vessel.

Composer, Janis Travis was interviewed by several media writers who had made the trip.

Janis had just completed her new composition, entitled "The Magic of his Caress".

In the piece she touches the emotions of her late husband's romantic caresses.

"I want the whole world to enjoy some of that passion that he had brought to our relationship. The musical interlude captures my special feelings for those caresses".

Her melodic composition was played each night by the performing groups on each level of the ship. Many people chose to dance to her delightful accomplishment.

Horace DeWinski, Vice Pres. of Porsche division of South American International Motors was busy working on his latest design for the 2028 Porsche Flying Sport drone.

He boasts that he has twelve individuals on his waiting list to buy the new model.

Samples of Chirardelli Chocolates of San Francisco were being given-away throughout the ship by representatives offering samples of several different delicacies.

Boston's non-profit "MassPort" was distributing vacuum-sealed cans of Boston Baked Beans.

The International Red Cross offered a gold chip to anyone giving a pint of blood, which became worth $100 US dollars at the ship's casino.

Although the New Titanic was not scheduled to stop in Nova Scotia, the journey was to take the ship reasonably close to that North American prominent location.

While in the area (although it was only April), they have planned to have Santa Claus visit the ship via helicopter bringing gifts to all passengers.

The gifts were to include the latest made personal umbrellas, attempting to help everyone to due their part to "keep Canada dry".

Also, ginger ale by the same catchy name would be freely offered to the viewing passengers while Santa was present.

The New Titanic Returns

Carl Mattore, Junior announced that his manure price had risen to $73 a ton, from $58. His brother-in-law (also aboard) reacted, "He's full of shit".

Somewhere on the vessel was Anita Smithson, aire to the Hula-Hoop empire of the 20th Century. Her uncle was Art Linkletter, a major investor in the invention itself (Note: Hoops were available at the clothing boutique @ $8 each).

The famous NYC Music Hall Rockettes could not make the trip, due to ongoing legal matters. However, the NYC Rockyettes, a Gay men's comedy group, dressed in female attire were present to hysterically butcher the famous routines at several locations throughout the journey. (Classic dance numbers were regularly performed.)

The late Rodney Dangerfield's step-uncle, Perce Dangerfield would slayed the people at the first-class midnight lounge. He rejected four-letter words and invented the five-letter ones that routinely "killed" his audiences.

Beth Wilcox from London each night was singing the spectacular tunes of Johnny Mercer, Irving Berlin, Duke Ellington, Harold Arlin, Rogers and Hart, Oscar Hamerstein, Peggy Lee, Mel Torme, Henry Mancini and Lois Vaughn. Her recordings gained International status when she hosted President Pense's inaugural.

The fragrance that most men love, Peanut Butter perfume was finally introduced to the public on the second day of the trip. Sample bottles were given to all the women, hoping to appease most of the men aboard who finally would have his lady wearing a fragrance that they (most men) enjoyed.

That new Canadian umbrella were being tested on the cold rainy upper deck. Santa's useful gift was being appreciated by those who received their samples.

Hollywood's latest movie, "The DuPont Robbery Nightmare", was being shown on all five floors at 8:00PM, on the third night at sea.

Coconut Soup was the specialty at dinner on the 3rd night. The shells were being stuffed with homemade cod fish sandwiches.

The Captain spoke on the ship's intercom announcing that the programed arrival in New York had been changed from 5:00PM to 2:00PM on the fifth day, due to the movement of the wind and sea.

He also announced that the ship's engines performances were beyond their expectations.

Boswell Peterson of Barcelona, Spain was six-feet, 10"tall.

He had eyes on Wendi Cegal.

They had met in line waiting for a lounge at the top deck.

Wendi was in-front with Boswell right behind her.

He began the conversation, "Say, I'm Boswell Peterson from Spain. Where are you from?"

The New Titanic Returns

"I'm an Ambassador to Paris. I'm on my way to New York to meet some family and friends. How about you?", she replied.

"I'm a basketball player, as you might guess by my size, I'm a member of the Lorin Tigers, of the Italian Men's Basketball League.

The Lorin Tigers is believed to be dedicated to Italy's famous movie star, Sophia no one can formally document that guess.

Anyway, my team got eliminated from the country's tournament and I'm free until October.

I thought this trip would give me an opportunity to see New York and parts of America. What about you?", he finished.

It was the beginning of a relationship that was to last until arriving in New York.

By mistake, an X-Rated movie was shown on the 3" level. Security was called in. The movie was confiscated. A John Wayne cowboy movie was the replacement.

On the third day, a reenactment of Lincoln's Gettysburg Address was delivered on the second level, beautifully performed in English and Spanish. Pop corn was given freely to everyone in attendance.

Pierre Bosh's romance became stronger.

They were meeting each evening in different locations.

He had verbally committed himself to divorce, promising her Georgina that he would begin legal proceedings, as soon as they reached New York.

Pierre also promised to meet with her regularly, to see if a future between them could be worked out.

They both were amazed at the common chemistry they appeared to have shared.

A long serious kiss ended each of their nightly meetings.

Diane Shlishkabob, Miss Ohio had accommodations on the second level.

She was runner-up in the Miss America Contest, coming in second to Miss Vermont, Sally O'Brien.

Diane was gorgeous, possessing measurements of 34-24-34.

Her boyfriend, Elliot Mash was an All-American Horseshoe Thrower, holding two world records, one for six straight "leaners", in World Competition, and one for beating six straight challengers in World Competition, two years in a row.

They had met at a New York Mets baseball game, back in 2021.

There was a clandestine poker game, developed on the second level. It was reported that one guy lost more than just his shirt.

Dining:

Turkey chips were served on each level every day, with different sauces that would change the wonderful tastes daily.

It became a favorite among the passengers.

Argentina's finest grilled steak had been highlighted at dinner the first evening.

French chicken (a-la Titanic), grilled with wine and mushrooms was served at dinner the second evening.

The third evening featured grilled Greek lamb and or grilled Atlantic salmon as an alternative.

There was more than plenty of booze, and magical drinks and no one could complain.

As expected, top rated food consumed a great portion of the total trip fee.

The culinary staff had come from several of the top schools from around the world.

No doubted that food management had become one of the most important areas that required the best in the planning of the ship's interior requirements.

An automated elevator was located at the stern end of the ship which traversed back-and-forth to all five floors.

Noise came from the elevator area on the third floor. Several individuals were running away from the location laughing and pointing as they ran.

It appeared that someone had passed gas in the elevator (farted).

The potent smell was rather discussing and several thought that someone had died in the elevator car itself.

Those waiting to use the elevator would not dare enter the unit.

(It could have been morning "sausages" and beans that were offered just an hour ago, at breakfast that had...to return to the atmosphere, as a punishment.

Someone reported the incident to the control room.

They announced on the public address speaker.... for passengers to avoid the third floor elevator area for an hour, at least.

When the announcement was finished, many people wondered what had happened there.

The New Titanic Returns

(To this date no one knows who the culprit had been.)

Jerimyra, the revolving robot would work his way around the top deck.

He would approach individuals asking if they needed drinks or other services. If anyone needed something he would communicate the request to the restaurant group, and server would quickly arrive.

Security didn't like the robot, because he would often push his way into a crowd to get attention and many people complained about his rudeness.

Often, Security would get the call or complaint and had to investigate, to calm down the people involved.

Jerimyra approached the thief, who was now incognito, with mustach, hat, glasses and a tailored suit., sitting by himself at a table on the top deck.

The robot pushed himself close to the thief. He didn't appreciate the gesture.

"Get out of here", he demanded. The robot began to offer his services.

The thief grabbed the robot and threw him backwards.

Jerimyra smashed against the cement floor.

Bells and voices started screaming at the thief.

Burt Jagolinzer

He quickly rose from his chair and started to run.

Carlton Mann was handcuffed to Captain Bert Williams of the Fall River, Massachusetts Police Department.

Captain Williams was a twenty-one-year veteran officer, who had flown to London to take control of Carlton Mann, who had escaped the United States. after stealing half-a-million dollars from the Fall River United Military Trust, six months ago.

It had taken six months to apprehend the thief, who had cleverly found his way to London to hide.

Scotland-Yard had located him and notified Fall River to come and get him.

They were bedded in the fourth level. Their instructions included not to visit the top level of the ship.

Security had been apprised of this arrangement.

Captain Bert Williams became sick and he was to be confined to bed on the second day.

He had called Security and arranged to have handcuff attached to the bathroom sink, so that he could remain in bed.

Carlton Mann saw this as a chance to escape.

The bottom of the sink had two pipes, and he thought he somehow break through one of the pipes and escape.

He would then hide the best he could on the ship.

Sure enough, Carlton Mann tugged on the pipes and wiggled one loose.

The Captain was sound asleep. He would go to the door and make his escape.

Carlton Mann was a veteran thief and tough guy.

He knew he had to avoid capture on the ship.

And so, he spotted a man walking in the corridor of the fourth level.

His name was Boris Helmbrecht, from Buffalo, New York, a machinist, who had been assigned to the Tool Room to help in emergency problems that could develop with the engines and operational equipment.

Carlton Mann approached him and pushed him into a corner.

"Lead me to your room... or I'll break your neck", Carlton demanded. "This way", Boris returned. They walked down the corridor to suite -411.

Boris took his key and they entered the room.

Carlton wacked him with his handcuffs. Boris fell to the rug.

He jumped on to Boris and choked him to death.

Getting up from the rug he sat down immediately at the room desk.

He began writing a letter addressed to Security and the Fall River Police.

(He would leave this letter in his own room, on the second level)

In the letter he admits to having robbed the bank and said he didn't want to spend years of his life in jail... and have decided to jump overboard to end his life. Sorry for your problems, Carlton

Carlton planned to throw Boris's body overboard that evening when it was dark.

He thought he could live in Boris's room for the remainder of the trip and avoid going to jail.

Maxwell Eisenhower, who was running for the U.S. Senate from Pennsylvania was busy working the ship looking for votes from anyone who would support his campaign.

As suspected, he was pleading for their financial contributions.

Maxwell was the first to run for political office, having attended four community colleges, three in Pennsylvania, one in Delaware. At this time, he had still no degrees and had finished high school, with three years of night school.

He admits he runs on his distant family name only. Maxwell had never married, but has four children (out of wedlock), two of which are currently in jail, on forgery charges.

The New Titanic Returns

Hollywood Producer Steven Sugarberg was searching the ship, looking for beauty and talent characters that could play roles in motion picture futures.

He had approached Pierre Bosh's girlfriend Georgina and offered her an audition after reaching New York.

She was flattered but didn't think she could enjoy working in the movie industry. (Besides, she was more interested in Pierre and a possible future with him).

Sugarberg kept going and landed a sixteen-year-old Ashley Cottenscarb, from Lucan Tennessee.

Pierre Bosh finally met up with Steven Sugarberg and the two of them hit it off quite well.

Bosh asked Sugarberg if he would like to partner with him to form The New Titanic Insurance Company, which would open it's door in New York.

They would make sure that they would initially be the insurance company of this ship when it continues it well-advertised runs, back-and-forth, Southampton to New York.

Sugarberg was delighted with the offer and they shook hands. They had agreed to each put up $25,000 to begin the corporation.

Nancy & Norma Burgess had purchased several items from the ship boutique and were enjoying the other amenities aboard the vessel.

There's an Oscar Mayor aboard who claims he is the Great-Grandson of the original Oscar Meyer, who is no longer alive.

This Oscar says that he changed his last name spelling to avoid any legal problems that might arise.

Several people think "He's full of Bologna".

Wine samplings were taking place throughout the trip. There were representatives from thirteen wineries of California, six from France, seven from Italy and eleven from Spain.

They all gave away samples at their respectful advertising stations along the rim of the far top deck.

A few drunks found their way to enjoy the continual freedom of the unlimited sample cups.

On the second level a meeting was taking place.

The Captain was discussing the active control report with two construction engineers, a member of the Finance Committee and a Britain Government Representative.

"Who's winning the soccer match with Arsonnel?", asked the Captain. "Due to a crack in the playing field area the event had to be postponed until May 7th", replied the British Representative.

One of the engineers began to speak, "There has been very little negative happenings aboard our craft. We're happy with all facets of operations.

Normal employee and security problems exist, but they are being addressed properly and should be resolved quite quickly"

After twenty minutes, discussing other minor matters the meeting was ended.

On the third day, third and fourth pick-pockets were reported.

Security people still had not located the thief. But they assured everyone that he (or she) would be arrested and brought to justice soon.

Arriving in New York:

The fifth and final day of the trip had arrived.

Captain Russ and the engineers were delighted with its performance. The craft had been built as a mighty vessel that could now continue to go back and forth across the great ocean, as intended.

They knew of no corrections or changes that would alter her next scheduled trip, returning to Southampton.

Ownership, investors and safety people have to be truly satisfied with her maiden voyage and could celebrate the completion of its initial goal.

Summary:

Peter Cummings (who had purchased the last ticket) had found new friendships with Nancy and Norma Burgess.

He had danced each night with both of them and romantically gave his best to each of them. They vowed to keep in touch after leaving the ship in New York.

Father Paul Grammitt enjoyed the cruise and was to be met by Rabbi Frank Goldman from New Jersey, who was to give him a complete tour of New York and meet three Cardinals, who were his personal friends.

Lional Zeel (from Russia), who had killed the room thief (instead of the pickpocketer) was turned over to the Russian Embassy in New York. His actions on the ship was to cause him to return to Russia (and probably face some sort of punishment).

Pierre Bosh and his wife left the ship without fanfare but their life together were to end quite quickly, now that their daughter had finally married. Pierre's girlfriend, Georgina would be waiting for his divorce to be completed, in hopes of beginning a future relationship with him.

The Fulla-Brush guy (Edmund Cool) made his quota and then some, going door to door. He was named salesman of the year by his company. Two years later he was to become Senior Vice President of Sales at the company.

Fifty-three-year-old Manny Fairfield was disenchanted with the trip. There was very little that he enjoyed. Manny wanted his money back and said he would never cruise again.

Amanda Stone and Billy-Bob Hudson had gotten married by Captain Russ on the last day of the trip. They phoned their friends and relatives and a great party was planned on the second day in New York.

Claude and Sarah Williamson, who had won the lottery decided to give each of their fourteen relatives $10,000 dollars. Sarah wants a larger diamond ring and Claude wants a sailboat.

Although Boswell Peterson, the basketball player, would have wanted a formal relationship with Wendi Cegall, she thanked him for his offer, but she would eventually go on to the Embassy in Paris, where she was directed by the Government.

Jules Madison, from Ireland had sold his citrus farm in Arizona but could not find a suitable woman that could enter his life. Yet, he enjoyed the historic trip and would return aboard her to Southampton.

The New Titanic Returns

Guido Barsorelli, the pick-pocket thief and murderer picked nine more pockets, while in disguise. His total take amounted to some three-thousand US dollars.

Even with one handcuff hidden in his jacket he was still capable to turn his trick.

Security had found his note in his room. But, they did not believe what he claimed to have done. They didn't think he would have left the ship.

Meanwhile the engine tool room reported their engineer missing. Security investigated immediately and began to piece the possible connection.

They knew where Boris's room was located. Security decided to storm Boris's room, expecting to find Guido, who was now linked to the disappearance of Boris.

With six individuals from Security, each with small armed guns, broke into Boris's room.

Guido had just taken his disguise off and was ready for bed. He gave up without a fight.

With still wearing a handcuff he was immediately supplemented with another cuff.

Guido never was to meet with the New York mob that was awaiting him and the special service that he was to employ during his limited stay in America.

In stead, Guido Barsorelli was charged with murder and multiple robberies. He was sentenced to life in jail by an International Court.

The money in his possession was given to local charities.

Author's Notes:

Although I tried to entertain while aboard the five days of the maiden voyage, I have chosen to insert limited views of the amenities aboard.
Hopefully you might have noted that I have done my best to set up the pre construction and bon voyage of the ship.
But, purposely I have left the unlimited logistics that it would ultimately take to plan and construct this gigantic undertaking... to the gifted individuals whose experience and educated knowledge would make this project beyond what I have described.
Sometimes crazy ideas influence challenges that better the world.

Burt Jagolinzer

LISTING OF THE CHARACTERS:
(In the order of their appearance within this novel)

1. Malcolm P. Iceberger, Chairman of White-Star Lines
2. Rosaline, Roz (Bosh) Gates
3. Terrance, Terry Gates
4. Pierre Bosh
5. Darlene Bosh
6. Jules Madison
7. Peter Madison
8. Juliette (O'Landy) Madison
9. Tigress Madison
10. Father Paul O'Grammit Manny Fairfield
11. Manny Fairfield
12. Caroline Fairfield
13. Claude Williamson
14. Sarah Williamson
15. Nancy Burgess
16. Norma Burgess
17. Captain Russell (Russ) Steinhoff
18. Peter Cummings
19. Wendi Cegall
20. Lianl Zeel

Intruduction:

The author in using his imagination presents a fictional happening aboard a new famous ship, during its proposed voyage across the seas.

All characters and incidents are totally the creation of the author.

Burt Jagolinzer has based his writings on the belief that a second Titanic could (and probably should) take place. Maybe the individuals that could organize such a challenge would be enticed by this author's idea and writing.

www.ingramcontent.com/pod-product-compliance
Lightning Source LLC
LaVergne TN
LVHW020423080526
838202LV00055B/5003